AF265517

A Family Magic Chapter Book

Spit Test

by Jennifer Lott
illustrated by Doriano Strologo

Spit Test
Book 3 of the Family Magic Series

Copyright © 2015 by Jennifer Lott

This is a work of fiction. Names, characters, places, and incidents are the products of the author's imagination or are used fictitiously and are not to be construed as real. Any resemblance to actual events, locales, organizations, or persons, living or dead, is entirely coincidental.

Reality Skimming Press
An Imprint of Okal Rel Universe
201-9329 University Crescent, Burnaby, BC, V5A 4Y4, Canada

Interior design: Lynda Williams
Cover & interior art: Doriano Strologo
ISBN: 978-0-9921402-8-1

All rights reserved. No part of this book may be reproduced, scanned, or distributed in any printed or electronic form without written permission. Please do not participate in or encourage piracy of copyrighted materials in violation of the author's rights. Purchase only authorized editions.

Library and Archives Canada Cataloguing in Publication

Lott, Jennifer, 1987-., author
    Spit Test / Jennifer Lott, Author; Doriano Strologo, Illustrator.

(Family Magic; 3)
ISBN 978-0-9921402-8-1 (pbk.)

    I. Strologo, Doriano, 1964-, illustrator II. Title.

PS8623.O87C87 2014   JC813'.6   C2014-900842-2

First Edition
(C-20140418)

Dedication

For my prepublication fans,
especially the children.

Visit the author's website at jenniferlott.com

Chapter 1

Charlotte didn't mind that her older sister Glenda was a witch. She didn't even mind that her mother was a witch. She didn't mind that she and her little sister Eileen had to wear wigs, while they waited for their magically removed hair to grow back.

No, after an uneventful week to think it all over…there was only one thing that *really* bothered Charlotte.

"A Spit Test!" cried Glenda. She had just spotted the potion recipe lying on the kitchen counter.

Charlotte held out a pickle jar. "Can you open this?"

Glenda took the jar and wrenched it open. "Why did you go looking for a Spit Test?"

Charlotte didn't answer. She dumped pickles into a big metal bowl.

Eileen came in from the backyard with a handful of black fluff. "Is this enough crow feathers?"

"I only need five." Charlotte snatched the feathers from her and counted.

Eileen peered into the bowl. "I think you put too much toothpaste in."

"I did not!" Furiously, Charlotte mashed gooey feathers and pickles together. She mashed until there were no more lumps.

For ten seconds, she stirred as fast

as her tired arms would stir.

She pointed into the finished potion and said, "Eileen, spit!"

Eileen spat into the bowl. The drop fizzed through the surface of the potion, making it pop like hot porridge. Charlotte waited for the fizzing to

stop. Then she elbowed Eileen out of the way. Charlotte spat. Her spit landed on top of the potion…and just lay there like a tiny puddle.

"That means you don't have natural magic," said Glenda.

"I know!" Charlotte had read all about the Spit Test on Glenda's computer. "Does everyone but me have magic on the inside?"

"Mom does," said Glenda.

Charlotte narrowed her eyes. "Do *you*?"

Glenda hesitated. "Well…"

"Spit!" Charlotte commanded.

Glenda did. The potion fizzed and popped like it had for Eileen.

"Charlotte," Glenda said quickly, "there are lots of spells you can do without natural magic."

Charlotte gritted her teeth. "If you and Eileen got natural magic from mommy…that must mean…”

Charlotte turned at the sound of their father’s wooden sandals tapping into the kitchen. She cannonballed into his stomach.

“Ooof!” he said. “Charlotte, what—”

“I have to test you.” She pointed him at the bowl. “Spit!”

His mouth made a big ‘O’ in his beard.

Glenda showed him the potion recipe.

Their father leaned over the bowl and spat. Nothing happened.

“You!” Charlotte’s head jerked up to glare at him. “You did this to me!”

“He can’t help his genes,” said

Glenda.

"He shouldn't have given them to me!" Charlotte stormed off.

"Charlotte!" Eileen ran up behind her and tugged on her arm. "You can use my spit for spells."

"I don't want *your* spit," she shouted. "I want *my* spit. I want magic spit too!"

Chapter 2

Getting ready to leave for school the next morning, Charlotte and Eileen took scarves out of the closet instead of hats. Pulling hats over top of their wigs made the wigs slip around.

"Mine still slips when I do this," said Eileen, shaking her head.

"Then don't do that," said Charlotte.

"But could you fix it?" Eileen asked eagerly. "Could you make mine stay on as good as yours?"

"You've got natural magic," said Charlotte. "You figure out how to do it."

They didn't talk in the van. They

just watched the snow banks go by outside the window and listened to their father whistling.

Charlotte was a bit happier at school with all her normal friends. Her friend Rachel knew that Glenda was a witch, but she didn't know about the Spit Test.

The minute they got home from school, Eileen asked their father, "When is mommy going to be home?"

"Not until late tonight, darling," he said.

"When is Glenda going to be home?" Eileen asked.

"Soon." He settled down on the couch for the beginning of his afterschool nap.

Charlotte was in the kitchen unpacking her lunch kit when she heard Glenda come in. She heard their father asking Glenda about her day.

Then Eileen was asking the questions. "If I want to do magic, do I have to spit on everything? Can I fix my wig that way? Charlotte said I should figure out how."

Charlotte froze. *Of course!* she thought bitterly, *Eileen has been waiting all day to ask one of the family witches about her specialness.*

"Magic spit is only for some spells and potions," said Glenda. "What you really have to find out is what your one natural power is."

Charlotte came back into the

living room.

"What's a natural power?" Eileen was asking.

"A magical ability that just happens in your brain, like…" Glenda stopped talking when she saw Charlotte.

Eileen didn't. "What's your natural power?"

"I don't know," said Glenda. "It hasn't happened yet."

"Do you have to be really old?" asked Eileen.

Charlotte slammed her backpack down in front of the closet.

Glenda looked at her for a few seconds, but then she said to Eileen: "It can happen anytime. It's different for different people."

"Has mommy's power happened yet?" asked Eileen.

"Yes," their father answered from the couch.

Charlotte kicked her backpack hard, forcing it past all the dangling coats in the closet.

"What's—" Eileen began.

"You know," Glenda interrupted, "it got so warm this afternoon, I only needed my sweater to walk home."

"Oh, I know," their father agreed. "It's only minus seven right now."

"So how about I take the Littles to the park?" Glenda offered.

Charlotte stamped her foot. "I don't want to be a Little anymore. I'm big enough to be a Medium!"

Chapter 3

The park was at the end of the alley next to their house.

The bright sun made the snow sparkle. Better yet, the lack of other people gave them the perfect opportunity for the shoe game. Glenda and Eileen pumped higher and higher on the swings. When they were high enough, they would draw a leg back and kick off one of their shoes.

Charlotte had to admit it *was* warmer this afternoon. She took off the stupid jacket she'd brought and tried to tie the sleeves around her waist. The sleeves were so poufy they barely left any ends to pull tight.

Glenda kicked her first boot just past the picnic table. She kicked her second boot so far past the merry-go-round that it hit a tree and bounced off.

"Come on, Eileen," said Glenda. "You're high enough."

Eileen squeezed her eyes shut. She kicked without wiggling, and her boot landed a few feet in front of the swing set. "I did it!"

"Big deal," said Charlotte. "You didn't even get to the picnic table."

"It was a good try," said Glenda.

"But I'll never get to play against Eileen, if you keep winning," said Charlotte.

"We don't have to play that way,"

said Glenda. "You play Eileen next."

"I don't want to," said Charlotte. "It's too easy to beat her."

"Charlotte—" Glenda began.

But Charlotte didn't want a lecture on how bad it was to hurt people's feelings. "I'm going home," she announced.

"But it's your turn to be the shoe collector," said Eileen.

"Get your own shoes with your fancy magic powers!" Charlotte marched down the snowy slope and into the alleyway that would take her home. Her poufy jacket lost hold of her waist and fell to the ground. She did not stop to pick it up.

"Oh!" Eileen kicked her second

boot forward at almost the right moment, so it almost made it to the picnic table. "I wish I *didn't* have a natural power."

"Don't say that." Glenda gripped the chains of her swing with her elbows to free her hands. She pointed at each of her distant boots.

Eileen watched as a few whispered words brought the boots soaring into Glenda's hands.

Glenda put her boots on, and got off the swing to collect Eileen's. "Our whole family can share magic. We don't all have to have it the same way."

"But Charlotte's brave," said Eileen. Her swing slowed. Her legs hung still and her chin drooped sadly.

"She should have a natural power to fight dragons or something."

"We don't have dragons in Prince George," Glenda pointed out.

"She's smart, too," said Eileen. "She should have a really smart power, like—"

"Like finding spells on my computer?" said Glenda.

"Yes, and saving me when you and mommy cast mean spells on us," said Eileen.

Glenda nodded. "Charlotte is feeling left out. We need to remind her that she's part of all this."

"But how?"

"Let's show her." Glenda went to pick up Charlotte's dropped jacket.

"Let's cast a spell."

Eileen felt much better now that they were helping Charlotte *and* still using magic.

Chapter 4

Charlotte was grateful she'd gotten most of her school work done earlier in the week. All the assignments she had to finish by Friday were called 'Must Do's. Today was Thursday, and the only thing she wanted to do was draw in her journal. She sat at a table beside Rachel, who was leaning over her own drawing, colouring it in.

Charlotte looked at Rachel's picture. It was a plate of half-eaten waffles appearing upside down on top of the computer desk in Rachel's living room. Rachel had also drawn Glenda as a cackling, green witch in a black pointed hat.

"Give her more warts," Charlotte advised.

"Good idea," said Rachel, adding dots to Glenda's face.

"I'm sorry Glenda cursed you," Charlotte said gloomily. "My family's really embarrassing."

*****

At recess, Charlotte found Eileen spreading embarrassment all over the playground.

"And then our hair was all over the house," Eileen babbled to a small, dark-haired girl, "and I saved the kitties, and—"

"Stop it!" Charlotte ran over. "No one will ever want to play with us again if you tell them that stuff!"

"It's okay," said Eileen, pulling her little friend forward. "Divya's family uses magic too."

Charlotte jumped. "Really?" She looked at the girl called Divya, who nodded.

Charlotte felt even worse.

More witches! Probably with more magic spit! She decided not to like Eileen's new friend.

Before she could say something unfriendly, Charlotte noticed what Eileen was holding. "What are you doing with my coat?" she asked.

"Oh, I was looking for you," said Eileen. "Here, put it on."

"I don't need it," said Charlotte.

"Good luck," Divya said to Eileen, and went to climb the monkey bars.

"What does that mean?" Charlotte said suspiciously.

"Here!" Eileen held the coat up high, trying to drop it on top of Charlotte's head.

Charlotte dodged. "When did you

meet Divya?"

"Five minutes ago," said Eileen. "Her daddy has natural magic and her mommy doesn't. That's like us only the other way around. Anyway, she doesn't know which one she is, so I thought she could come to our house and—"

"And spit in our potion?" Charlotte made a face. "No way! Let her make her own Spit Test."

"They don't have the recipe," said Eileen.

"Then how did her dad find out *he* had natural magic?"

"He just waited until the first time that his power happened. The very first time it does, birds fly out from the palms of your hands."

Charlotte snorted.

"No, it's true," Eileen insisted.

The bell rang.

Charlotte was turning away, when Eileen ran at her with the coat.

The sleeves caught on Charlotte's fingers and slid up her arms back-to-front. The zipper flapped open behind her, but she couldn't shake the coat off. The sleeves were *stuck* on her arms!

"What did you do?" Charlotte whirled on Eileen. "Get it off me!"

"I'm not supposed to!" Eileen took off for class.

Charlotte thrashed inside her sleeves. In a few seconds, the clinging coat slid off again.

Charlotte gasped. Her arms felt

tingly.

She pushed her long sleeves up as high as they would go, and screamed. Skinny, sparkly worms wiggled under her skin. They were *inside* her arms!

She pulled her sleeves back down quickly. A teacher was calling her back into school.

Chapter 5

Charlotte went in the wrong door. She passed the Kindergarten classroom instead of the one next to hers.

Only one little boy was still out in the hall. He was the shortest

Kindergartener she'd ever seen. He jumped up and down in front of the coat rack, trying to get his bag to go on top.

"Here, let me do it." Charlotte took his bag from him and lifted it easily to the top of the rack. One of her arms prickled. "Ah!"

"Thanks," the little boy said, not noticing. He went into his classroom.

Charlotte pulled back the sleeve of her prickling arm. Some worms wiggled into new shapes. Worms twisted together, or broke apart, or straightened…in a moment three strange words were there in her skin. Charlotte couldn't understand them. The prickling stopped, and the leftover worms went back to small wiggle movements.

Charlotte shivered and looked away. "Ohhh…this can't be good." She rubbed nervously at the words on her arm.

A boot she was looking at flew up to the ceiling.

Charlotte yelped. She clutched her arm harder, eyes darting everywhere.

She saw snow pants: they flew up! She saw a hat: up it went! She squeezed her prickling arm and saw a lunchbox fly. The ceiling light was getting covered with stuff, and the hallway was getting darker.

"What's all this noise?" The Kindergarten teacher was coming out.

Charlotte let go of her arm and ran.

"You're late," said Ms. Yancy, when Charlotte tore inside her classroom.

"I had a good reason!" Charlotte panted.

She decided not to explain further. She showed Ms. Yancy all the 'Must Do's she'd ticked off, and escaped to a table to read books.

Rachel joined her, labelling a map and eating a fruit roll-up.

"You're not supposed to eat at your work space," Charlotte reminded her.

"I was too busy playing at recess," Rachel explained.

"Don't let Ms. Yancy see."
Charlotte propped her books up in front

of Rachel, hiding the snack from view.

Charlotte's other arm prickled. "No, no, no…" she said under her breath.

"What?" Rachel whispered.

"It's worm-words again!" Charlotte rolled back her sleeve. Sure enough, new words were forming in her skin.

Rachel's big brown eyes got wider. "What did your sister do this time?"

"I'm not really sure," said Charlotte. There were four strange words on her arm this time. Again, she couldn't read them. But she touched them. When she touched them, she was looking at Rachel's fruit roll-up.

The fruit roll-up disappeared.

"Hey!" Rachel stared at the air between her fingers. She squeezed and her fingers got no closer together. "It's still here!"

Charlotte reached out and felt the sticky snack in Rachel's hand. It *was* there. Invisible!

Charlotte flattened her books on the table. "Well," she said shakily to Rachel, "you can eat it now."

Chapter 6

That afternoon, Charlotte snuck into Eileen's classroom.

On a floor mat, Eileen was stacking cubes made of golden beads. Each cube represented a thousand. Charlotte remembered using the same materials when she learned to do math problems with big numbers.

"One thousand, two thousand, three thousand," Eileen counted as she stacked three cubes on top of each other.

Charlotte dropped to her hands and knees in front of her.

Eileen looked up with a start.

"You have to come with me," Charlotte whispered. "It's an emergency!"

Eileen wrote her name under the washroom sign on the chalkboard, and walked out of class.

In the hall, Charlotte rolled up her sleeves to show Eileen both arms. "Look what you did. Worms are spelling all over me!"

"Oh..." Eileen leaned over the

wormy words, fascinated.

Charlotte scowled. "You messed with magic you don't understand, and now we have to—"

"I didn't!" Eileen cried. "Glenda understands the spell."

Charlotte's jaw dropped. "This was

Glenda's idea?"

"Yes," said Eileen. "It's a good spell."

"Glenda never casts good spells on us," said Charlotte.

"This is her first one," Eileen admitted.

"I can't believe you helped her."

Eileen looked down at the floor. "It's to help *you*," she said in a small voice.

Charlotte glared at her. "You're turning evil now that you've got magic spit."

"No, I'm not!" said Eileen, starting to get upset. "Glenda said our whole family is going to be good witches now."

"I'm not a real witch and neither is daddy!" she shouted.

"But," Eileen sniffed, "Glenda said—"

"You can't listen to…oh…Eileen, don't cry."

Without thinking about the spells in her arms, Charlotte gave her little sister a hug. The worm-words didn't stick to Eileen. She wiped her eyes and hugged back.

"You just shouldn't listen to Glenda," Charlotte explained in a quieter voice. "Or mommy. They're both *mean* witches."

She gave Eileen an extra squeeze before letting go.

"There's another one!" Eileen

cried, pointing.

Charlotte looked down. Another curly line of words went still below her elbow. Too curious to resist, she tapped the new words.

A small cloud popped into the air and settled on her chest. It didn't feel wet, like a real cloud would feel. It was soft and warm.

Charlotte took the cloud in her arms and held it in front of her. It felt so comfy. At home, she'd be tempted to curl up on the couch with it.

"It…it is a weird thing for a mean witch to do," she admitted.

"I told you!" Eileen said triumphantly.

Charlotte sighed, batting the

warm cloud away. "But these spells got *attached* to me. I'm still not a real witch."

"Yes, you are," Eileen insisted. "Glenda said good witches *earn* the spells. That's what you're doing."

"Really?" Charlotte said, doubtfully.

But later, when Eileen had returned to class, Charlotte touched the cloud spell on purpose. She was at the bathroom sink. As it turned out, her new comfy cloud was the perfect way to dry her hands.

48

Chapter 7

By the end of the school day, Charlotte had learned to be very careful about touching the first two spells on her arms. She made sure she looked at the right object at the right moment.

In the van, she sent a juice box floating up to the ceiling.

"Charlotte!" her father barked. "No magic while I'm driving. It's very distracting."

"Okay." Charlotte tapped her other arm to make the juice box invisible.

The van pulled into their driveway.

Charlotte looked at her arms. "Oh no!" she gasped.

The words were beginning to fade. She tapped them all, but they only seemed to fade faster.

"Hurry up." Her father jangled the key he needed to lock the van. Eileen was already out.

Charlotte didn't move. "I'm losing them, daddy."

"Losing what?" he asked.

"The spells!" She held out her arms.

"Glenda said they wouldn't stick the whole day," said Eileen.

"No!" Charlotte cried. "I wanted to use them again ton—"

"Then write them down," said her father.

Charlotte hadn't thought of this.

By the time she got to the dining room table with paper and pencil, the words on her arms were very faint indeed. She copied them down as fast as she could.

Meanwhile, Eileen curled up on the couch with a stapled printout that Glenda had given her: <u>Domestic Witchcraft for Ages 6-12</u>.

Charlotte tapped the words she'd written on the paper, but nothing happened.

"I think you'll have to *say* the words now," her father said, coming up behind her.

"I can't," she told him. "It's an impossible-to-say magic language."

"Oh, no, it's not," he said, sounding surprised. "That's German."

She looked round at him. "It is?"

"Yes. I learned German while I was living in Austria." He pointed at

one of the spells. "That one you say: *H-ueh-her als ik!*" He made a throaty noise at the end. "It means—"

"No, daddy!" Eileen scurried over from her corner. "If you tell us what they mean, they won't work anymore."

He blinked at her.

"It says so." She held out her printout. "That spell you just said is one that I can't cast in French, because I already learned what the French words mean. Every language uses different words for the same spell, so you can cast the spell no matter what language you understand, you see?"

Her father shook his head, looking bewildered.

"Watch." Eileen held a pencil in front of her eyes and said to it, "*Au-delà de ma hauteur*!"

Nothing happened.

Eileen nodded proudly. "*H ö h e r als ich*!" she cried instead.

The pencil rose like a helium balloon and stuck in the ceiling.

"So German won't work for me?" Her father tried the spell that way on a pen. The pen didn't move.

"You can use the French one!" Eileen

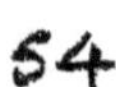

squealed, pushing the printout into his free hand.

"*Au-delà de*," he read slowly, "*ma hauteur!*"

The stapled papers under his gaze shot up to the ceiling

and stayed there.

Eileen gave him a reproachful look. "I was still reading that, daddy. How do we get it down?"

Chapter 8

That evening, Charlotte was allowed in Glenda's room to use Glenda's computer. Charlotte meant to find a 'down' spell and a 'visible' spell to undo all the spells everyone had cast, but she forgot about this when she found a new book of potion recipes. For half an hour, she double clicked on documents. For another ten minutes, she sent documents to the printer in the living room.

The last recipe she found was headed 'Taste Dip':

Dip any food in this to make it taste and feel like your favourite food. Dipped food keeps its original appearance and nutrients.

To make a Taste Dip, mix together in a bowl:

-1/4 cup salt

-1/4 cup sugar

-1/4 cup lemon juice

-1/4 cup black coffee

-2 cups of the desired food flavour (for best results, condense the food itself into powder, paste or juice)

Charlotte was already imagining what she could prepare: 2 cups of melted chocolate, 2 cups of cheesy popcorn crumbs, 2 cups of squished gummy bears – she could make a dip for every meal tomorrow!

There was only one more line in the recipe. She was halfway out of her seat, when she noticed it. Her heart sank.

Add 1 teaspoon of natural witch saliva.

"Nooo!" She dropped into the chair and slammed her hand down on the mouse. She clicked open each of the recipes she'd printed. She read them more carefully.

'TinHeart Oil' that made toys dance…no problem. 'Bob Foam' that made heavy things float…good to go. She went on checking and counting. Thirty other potions ready to be brewed.

Glenda was right. Most potions didn't need magic spit. Taste Dip – the *best* one – did need it!

"You have to put more paper in the printer," Glenda's voice called from the hall.

"Grrr!" said Charlotte.

"What?" Glenda came in. "Need help with something?"

Charlotte stuck her nose in the air. "No. Keep your yucky spit to yourself."

"Ah." Glenda went out again and came back with the pages Charlotte had printed. "Do you think you'll be good at making potions?"

"Yes," said Charlotte. "I made the Spit Test right the first time."

Glenda stapled the pages.

Charlotte stared at the computer screen. She turned her head when her

big sister waved a hand in front of her face.

"If you make a yucky potion full of super cool magic," said Glenda, "I won't tell you to keep it to yourself. Share, share, share!"

"No tickling!" Charlotte ducked as Glenda's fingers went wiggling for her armpits.

"I'm *sharing* tickles!"

"No, no, no—" Interrupted by her own laughter, Charlotte tickled back.

Glenda tried not to laugh. "Too much sharing!" she wheezed.

"Tell me about it," said Charlotte, thinking about spit again.

Chapter 9

After Friday at school, Charlotte tried not to think about magic at all. *Nothing wrong with a nice, normal day,* she decided, *at least once in a while.*

Classes got out early for extra playground time. Charlotte walked around the school. Before she could get to the nice, normal jungle gym, she saw something that changed her plans.

Eileen was backed into a corner — a corner in an undercover part of the playground where kids played pavement games. There were kids there now. Kids laughing at Eileen...Eileen without her wig!

"Give it back," said a serious little voice that wasn't Eileen's.

Too far to one side to see the whole space, Charlotte backed up for a wider view.

Divya was in the same corner. She was asking a boy with Eileen's wig in his hand to 'give it back.' Divya was being very shy, so the boy was ignoring her.

Eileen had pulled her scarf up over the short fuzz on her head. In a panicky voice, she told the other kids about how she lost her hair. When she got to the part about using her own spit to grow it back, the laughter got much worse.

Charlotte circled to the side of the

group where no one was looking.

"Go ahead," the kids urged Eileen. "Make your hair grow back now."

"I can't!" Eileen tried to tell them. "If I do, my hair will never stop growing. It's very dangerous."

They laughed.

Charlotte walked faster.

"She's telling the truth," said Divya.

"Oh, yeah," laughed the tallest girl, "like when she said spells only work if you don't know what they mean! Oogoo boofoo – there, I cast a spell."

"Who invented them?" laughed the boy with Eileen's wig. "The Tooth Fairy?"

Charlotte snatched the wig from him before he noticed her. "It still has to be the *right* words, of course!" she shouted at the laughing kids. "Just like ingredients in a recipe. And I don't know *who* made all the spells, but they *do* work, and you're *not* making fun of my little sister anymore!"

"She can't do magic," said the tallest girl. "All she does is talk about it."

"She just doesn't want to scare you, because she's nicer than me!" Charlotte looked for bags lying at the kids' feet. She pointed at a backpack, and cried, "*Augen sehen Sie nicht!*"

The backpack disappeared. Actually, it was just invisible.

The screaming kids didn't realize this. A few of them tripped over the backpack, as they rushed to get away from Charlotte's pointing finger.

"Oh!" Eileen grabbed her big sister's arm, looking excited and worried at the same time. "What if they tell on you?"

"Ha!" said Charlotte. "Let them try."

Eileen took her wig back with a watery smile.

"Come on, Divya," said Charlotte, turning to her. "Let's go ask our daddies if you can come over to play."

"I have to ask my mommy," said Divya. "She picks me up."

"Weird," said Charlotte.

Chapter 10

Glenda took Charlotte, Eileen and Divya to the park. Charlotte played against Divya on the swings. It was Eileen's turn to be the shoe collector.

Glenda was lookout. "Kids coming to the park gate," she warned. "If they want to play in front of the swings, you'll have to stop kicking your shoes off."

Charlotte sat tall on her swing to look. The kids were chatting and hurrying over to play. Charlotte linked her elbows around her swing chains, and pointed at them. *"Gib uns mehr Zeit!"*

The kids walked slower. Their feet dragged step…by step. They still talked fast, and didn't seem to notice how much slower their bodies were moving.

Glenda grinned at Charlotte. "You cast that really well."

"Daddy says it better," Charlotte admitted. "Did you know he speaks one of the magic languages fluently?"

Glenda nodded. "That's why I cast all my spells in German."

Charlotte's heart leapt. "You mean *you* needed daddy for your spells?"

"Yep." Glenda laughed. "I had to ask him how to pronounce everything, before he even knew about magic."

Charlotte swung up high and kicked her shoe over the merry-go-round.

*****

When Divya came home with them, Charlotte and Eileen took her to their mother's windowless office in the basement.

"Don't worry," said Eileen.

"Mommy's still at work."

"I left the Spit Test on top of her cauldron," Charlotte explained.

The three of them stepped inside the office. They heard the *tap, tap, tap* of wooden sandals on the basement floor.

"Daddy's coming!" Eileen closed the door after them in a hurry.

The office went pitch black.

Divya gave a frightened yelp. "I don't like the dark," she said.

"Sorry!" Eileen felt around for the string to pull the ceiling lamp on.

Suddenly, the lamp wasn't necessary. Four bright lights, close together, switched on.

Charlotte shielded her eyes to

look at Divya. The lights were coming from Divya's elbows and knees.

"Who said that spell?" Charlotte began. "I didn't hear—"

But then she saw the flock of tiny, red-breasted robins bursting from Divya's hands. They flew up all at once. Then they faded away, like tricks on the eyes.

Divya looked amazed. The lights

at her elbows and knees shone on. It was as if her brain had sent a message to four flashlights inside of her.

"Wow," breathed Eileen.

Charlotte thought about how little birds would fly out of her sisters' palms someday. The first time their natural powers happened, would they become lazy witches and stop learning new words and potions? Would they forget that their father had no natural magic, but could still teach them every spell in Glenda's books?

No matter what they do, sisters are sisters, Charlotte decided, *and I just won't let natural magic make them lazy and forgetful.*

Charlotte smiled at Divya. New

friends were new friends, too.

"Never mind testing your spit," she told the glowing girl. "Can I use some to make Taste Dip potions?"

www.ingramcontent.com/pod-product-compliance
Lightning Source LLC
Chambersburg PA
CBHW061044050726
47592CB00004B/1589